CHAPTER 1 AND L.A.P.
Renton School District 403

Lily, the Lovable Lion

by NORMAN BORISOFF

SPRINT BOOKS

SCHOLASTIC BOOK SERVICES
New York   Toronto   London   Auckland   Sydney   Tokyo

Design/Karen Beckhardt
Illustrations/Jos. A. Smith

Copyright © 1975 by Norman Borisoff. All rights reserved. Published by Scholastic Book Services, a division of Scholastic Magazines, Inc.

Printed in the U.S.A.

13 12 11 10 9 8 7 6 5 4   8 9/7 0 1 2/8
                                                                          09

"The Greatest Little Travel-
ing Circus in the World!" That's what the sign
said. It was little, all right, but it sure wasn't
great.

We went to the Grand Opening. Me, my sister
Susan, and my brother Pete. By the time it was half
over, I was ready to go home. I had seen better
acts on TV a hundred times. But I couldn't leave
because of Susan and Pete.

You see, Susan is 12, and Pete is only nine. I'm
14 — the oldest. I had told my folks that I would
look after them. Susan and Pete wanted to see the
last number on the bill: "Fearless Freddie and His
Man-Eating Animals."

Before Freddie's act, all the lights were turned

off and a spotlight came on. It was shining down on a big cage. Fearless Freddie and two men were wheeling the cage into the middle of the ring.

There were four animals in the cage — two tigers and two lions. There were also four small stands.

The animals were roaring. The noise was so loud that the walls of the tent seemed to shake.

For the first time that evening, we all sat up and watched. We were going to see something for our money, at last.

The noise died down. Then there was a long, slow roll of drums.

Fearless Freddie, wearing what looked like an

old bearskin, took a bow. One of his men handed him a long whip.

Freddie turned to the crowd and said:

"Ladies and Gentlemen! I will walk in the cage of these man-eating animals. I will not be afraid. I will be their master!"

There was another sound of drums. Freddie bowed again. The crowd applauded. Those animals looked big enough to be dangerous. And they sounded pretty wild.

Freddie waved to his men. They opened the door just wide enough for him to step in. Then they shut the door and backed away. They seemed afraid that the wild animals would tear them to

pieces. The show was beginning to get good.

Freddie took two steps. The animals moved away from him. Some of them had their mouths open. We could see their sharp teeth.

But Freddie seemed as fearless as his name.

He lifted that mean-looking whip and snapped it. It made a noise like two pistol shots. The animals backed up against the far wall.

"Ho! Ho! My wild friends," yelled Freddie. "You can't get away from me. You are here to do what I say."

He looked around at the four big cats. "You first," he said, pointing to one of the tigers. "Tom the Terror!"

Tom the Terror got down on his back legs. He was ready to spring. Freddie cracked the whip.

Tom let out a roar and jumped — clear across the cage.

Freddie ducked, then he went after Tom. "Up on your stand," he shouted. "And I mean right now!"

Freddie lifted the whip again. Tom watched him, waiting for the next move. Then, all of a sudden, Tom climbed up on one of the little stands. Just like that.

I looked at Susan. She was looking at me. I could tell we were both thinking the same thing. Tom the Terror looked more like a scared kitten than a wild tiger.

Freddie went back to the center of the cage. He took a bow. Only a few people in the crowd applauded. But Freddie didn't seem to notice. He started his next number with the other tiger — "Mary the Marauder."

It was the same thing. Mary ran around a little bit, then she stopped and climbed up on a chair. This time practically no one applauded. But it didn't seem to bother Freddie at all. He just smiled and said:

"I will now work with the most dangerous animal on earth. The lion!"

He cracked his whip at a big lion. "Come on, Louie!" he said.

Louie backed away. Freddie followed him. Louie growled and ran across the cage. Freddie turned and swung the whip. You could hear the noise as it landed on Louie's back.

Louie let out a howl and raced around the cage. Freddie raced after him, cracking the whip. Louie kept running, and Freddie kept running after him.

Louie let out what sounded like a cry. Then he climbed up on his stand. This time, not one person applauded.

Pete turned to me and Susan. "That lion is not dangerous. None of these animals are. Fearless Freddie is a fake! Just look at that poor lion. He's all out of breath!"

It was true. Louie was breathing hard like a very old lion.

"Well, don't tell me," I told Pete. "You were the one who wanted to stay for this act."

"I thought it would be exciting," said Pete.

"Exciting," said Susan. "It's about as exciting as making fudge!"

I didn't say anything. I was just waiting for Freddie's number to be over, so we could leave.

Little did I know that the most exciting part of the evening was yet to come!

CHAPTER 2

Freddie took a short break to catch his own breath. One of his men handed him a glass of water, slipping it between the bars.

I guess that's when I knew that Freddie's whole act was a real fake. The animals were all sitting and resting. But the roaring went on. It wasn't coming from the animals at all. It was coming from the loudspeakers! That scary noise was on a record.

Freddie handed the glass back to one of his men. Then the noise stopped so that Freddie could give another one of his little talks.

"Now, I have a question for you," he said to the crowd. "If the lion is the most dangerous animal on earth, what in the world could be more deadly?"

For a few seconds, there was silence. Then a man in the crowd called out: "A phony animal-tamer! With an act like yours, we could all be bored to death!"

The crowd laughed, but Freddie kept his cool. "Very good, very good," he said, smiling. "I'll have to use that line in my act some day. But I'm sure that some of the men here know the answer," he went on. "With animals — as with humans — the female is deadlier than the male."

"This guy is really dumb," said Susan.

Freddie turned to the other lion. "Lethal Lily, the Queen of Killers!"

Lily had not moved since Freddie stepped into the cage. She looked so old and tired, I couldn't see her killing a mouse. Even from where we were sitting, we could see her bones. We could tell she didn't get enough to eat.

Freddie snapped his whip.

Lily didn't move.

Freddie came a little nearer, whipping her again.

Lily still didn't move.

"She is trying to get me to come closer," Freddie told the crowd. "She would like a nice bite out of my arm. All right, Lily," he said. "Here!"

He pushed his whip hand close to Lily's face. Lily backed away.

Then Freddie cracked her on the head with the end of the whip. Really hard!

A few people booed. The other animals in the cage started to growl. It wasn't the loudspeakers this time. But Lily didn't move or make a sound.

"Get up on your stand, Lily!" yelled Freddie, losing his temper and hitting her again and again.

Lily let out a moan and dropped to the floor.

Freddie seemed to go out of his mind. He started beating and whipping Lily. The crowd was booing, whistling, and yelling. Some people were climbing over the rail and into the ring.

In the cage, the other animals got off their stands. They started moving toward Freddie. They were roaring — FOR REAL!

Fearless Freddie was terrified. "Get this cage out of here!" he cried to his men. "And get me out of it!"

In the excitement that followed, somebody put some music on the loudspeakers. But no one remembered to turn on the lights.

People were running around in the dark. Freddie's men were dragging the cage out of the tent. Freddie was screaming at them to open the cage and let him out. And the animals were roaring louder than ever.

"This whole show is a fake," someone said. "Where is the manager? We want our money back!"

The place was turning into a madhouse. I took Susan with one hand and Pete with the other.

"Let's get out of here," I told them. "We might get hurt."

I spotted a hole in the tent, and we headed for it fast. But once we got outside, Pete stopped me. "We should try to get our money back, too," he said.

"Forget it," I told him, pulling him away.

Pete started to argue, but Susan shut him up. "Glenn is right," she said. "Let's just go home and forget the whole thing."

Well, we went home. But we didn't exactly forget it.

For one thing, we all heard about the big riot that followed. For another, we saw the circus wagons leaving Millburg that same night.

But no one even dreamed that this was only the beginning of the strangest thing that ever happened to all of us. . . .

CHAPTER 3

The next day was Saturday. No school. If it had been a weekday, this whole thing might never have happened. But on Saturday mornings, my friends and I always play ball in the park. I'll never forget that day — or that game.

The other team was leading, right into the last inning. We got two runs and tied the game up. Then both teams went neck-and-neck for five more innings. Finally, we made the winning run!

We all crowded around the hot dog stand to celebrate. I was just biting into a nice, juicy frank, when Susan came along. She was all excited.

"You know what time it is?" she asked. "Mom is getting worried."

I told her what a close game it had been.

"Well, you better come home," she said, not interested.

I dug out some extra change to buy her a frank, too. She didn't want one. She wanted an ice cream cone. So I bought her one, and we started home together.

Because it was late, we took the shortcut. It goes along a little river — a brook, really — and then over a big pile of rocks. As we got to the top of the rocks, Susan stopped.

"Do you hear that, Glenn?" she asked.

I stopped and listened. There was a funny sound

coming from somewhere around us. It sounded like somebody crying. Only — no one was around!

We looked and we looked, but we couldn't see a thing. But we kept on hearing the sound. It was sort of spooky.

"It seems to be coming from somewhere down there," I said. Susan thought so, too. So we climbed back down.

We looked all around those rocks. There was no one in sight. But as we followed the sound, we got closer and closer to the water. Then I saw something I had never seen before. On the river side of the rock pile, behind some bushes, was a hole.

And that's where the sound was coming from!

"Be careful!" said Susan, as I made my way along the edge of the river. "You'll get your sneakers wet."

I was so careful that I didn't know Susan was right behind me. I was excited — and nervous. That hole had to be the entrance to a cave. And whoever was crying was inside it.

I poked my head in. It was a cave, all right! But it was so dark I couldn't see a thing. A few seconds later, I could feel Susan crawling in behind me. She couldn't see anything, either. Then, all of a sudden, we were both scared stiff.

I could feel goose pimples all over me. At the same time, the crying stopped. I didn't know what to make of it.

To tell the truth, I felt like getting out of that place and running for my life. But I was so scared I couldn't move.

The sound of crying started again. At the same time, a pair of green eyes began to come closer.

I tried to call out to Susan. I opened my mouth, but no words came out. And, before I could make a move, I heard Susan gasp, "It's a lion!"

At that, the eyes stopped moving. But, by this time, I could see for myself that they belonged to a lion. And I guessed — I don't know how — that this wasn't just any lion. It was Lily — from the circus!

All of a sudden, I had the feeling that Lily was just as scared as we were. I took a chance and said, as softly as I could, "Hi, Lily."

Animals understand a lot of things. Don't ask me how, but they do. And when Lily heard my voice, she started to purr. Just like a big cat. Then she came right over to us.

From that minute on, I knew she wouldn't hurt us. So I petted her and said a few things, the way you talk to a dog or a cat. Lily purred some more.

Susan also petted her. Lily really seemed to know that we felt friendly.

"I wonder how she got here," said Susan.

I was thinking the same thing. "Maybe she escaped during the riot," I said.

"I don't blame her," said Susan. "The way that mean, rotten Freddie treated her."

By now, our eyes were used to the dim light of the cave. We could see marks on Lily's skin from the whipping and beating. Two big tears rolled down from her eyes.

"She must be badly hurt," I told Susan.

Susan nodded. "And I'll bet she is hungry." Then, almost without thinking, she held out her ice cream cone to Lily.

I wanted to tell Susan that lions don't eat ice cream. But, before I could get the words out, Lily opened her mouth and swallowed the whole thing!

"She is starving," said Susan. "Let's get her something to eat."

I thought that was a great idea. I never dreamed what a problem it would turn out to be.

We told Lily to stay there and keep quiet. We would be back soon with some food. I knew she

couldn't understand the words. But I hoped she would get the message. Then we left and ran home.

I checked in with Mom, so she wouldn't worry. I made up a story about having another ball game that afternoon. Then I went to my secret hiding place where I keep my paper-route money. I took some money. I also got my flashlight. I thought I might need it.

Susan and I went to the store and bought a pound of hamburger. Then we raced back to the park.

When we got to the cave, we could hear Lily crying again. But she stopped the minute she heard us. We crawled inside. Susan held the flashlight, while I opened the package.

"We brought you some food, Lily," I said, putting the meat under her nose. Before I could say another word, she gobbled it all up! Chomp! Just like that.

I couldn't believe my own eyes. "Man," I told Susan, "if a pound of meat is only one mouthful — we're in trouble!"

"Maybe," Susan said slowly, "it's just because she didn't eat anything all day."

"Maybe," I said, worried. "But it's going to cost us to find out."

I never dreamed how much it would cost before it was all over.

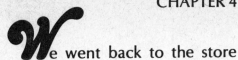e went back to the store and bought another pound of hamburger. Lily swallowed it like a cracker! Then we bought two more pounds. Lily swallowed that in two bites. Chomp! Chomp!

I was beginning to run out of money. "We will have to find some cheaper way to feed her," I told Susan.

"Don't worry," she said. "We will."

I hoped so. But that didn't stop me from worrying. We told Lily to take it easy. We promised to come back and see her tomorrow. Then we went home.

All through dinner, I kept thinking about how to

feed Lily. But it was Susan who thought of a way to do it.

"We will do the dishes tonight," she said as we were getting up from the table.

Mom gave us a funny look and said, "All right, if you want to."

Susan scraped all the plates. But instead of throwing the leftovers into the garbage can, she put them in a plastic bag. She saved everything: little bits of meat, potatoes, vegetables, and salad. She even poured the gravy into that bag.

"I get the idea," I told Susan. "But I wonder if it will work. Lions like meat."

"But they like other things, too," said Susan. "She ate my ice cream cone. Remember?"

I remembered. And I hoped Susan was right. Anyway, we had nothing to lose by trying. The only trouble was that there were not too many leftovers. The whole bag only weighed about a pound. One mouthful for Lily.

I pointed this out to Susan. Then I had an idea. I decided to do a little work for Mom, too. I went through the refrigerator and cleaned out all the leftovers I could find there.

By the time we were through, the bag weighed around four pounds. We couldn't wait to see how Lily would feel about this meal the next day.

We should not have worried. Lily gobbled up everything. She kept licking the bag, and we could see she was still hungry. Susan and I looked at each other.

"How much does a lion eat?" asked Susan.

I shook my head. I didn't know. In fact, I didn't know anything about lions. "We should try to find out," I told her. "Soon!"

Susan agreed. "We could get a book out of the library."

"It's Sunday," I told her. "The library is closed."

Then I thought of something else. Even though Millburg is only a small town, the park is pretty big. It has a pond, with ducks and swans. And there is a stable for horse rides. An old man, Ollie Olson, takes care of the horses and feeds the ducks and swans. Maybe he knew something about lions.

We found Ollie with the horses. He seemed surprised by our questions.

"It is for a school project," Susan said.

"Well, let's see," said Ollie, scratching his head. "I used to work in a zoo. And we had some lions. We used to feed them ten to twelve pounds of horsemeat a day. Each!"

"Horsemeat!" I cried out, before I could stop myself. "Where do you get horsemeat?"

Ollie gave us a funny look. "You two planning to adopt a lion?" he asked.

"Oh, no!" Susan told him. "It's just that we have to write this report. So we wanted the whole picture."

31

Ollie shook his head. "I don't know where you could buy horsemeat around here. But they will eat other kinds of meat, too."

Well, we sure got the whole picture. I could just see myself buying Lily ten to twelve pounds of meat every day! That would cost more than my mother spends to feed the whole family!

By the time we left Ollie, I was feeling so low that I just couldn't face Lily. Not right away. "Let's go have a Coke," I told Susan. She was all for it.

We went to Red's Diner, which is right across the street from the park. I ordered two Cokes. While we were sitting there thinking about Lily, an idea jumped into my head.

To tell the truth, it was the same idea Susan had the night before, at home. But there were only five people in my family. Red had lots of customers — and lots of leftovers!

I waited until business slowed down a little. At the same time, I worked out a story. When Red was free, I caught his attention. I tried to sound real cool and serious.

"I was just wondering," I told him, "what you do with all that leftover food you throw out."

Red's eyes blinked. "What do you mean — what do I do with it? I throw it out — just like you said. Why?"

"We have a gardening project at school. And

that stuff would be great for a compost heap."

"What is a compost heap?" Red wanted to know.

"Just that. A lot of old food that you spread over the ground. It mixes with the soil. Makes it very good for growing things."

"You mean you want some of that garbage?" asked Red.

"It's only garbage if you throw it out," I said. I felt very proud to come up with that answer. "But it's food for the soil, if you use it right."

"The barrels weigh over 50 pounds. How are you going to move them?" Red asked.

Susan said, "We could just take a little bit every day. Ten or twelve pounds."

"And mess up my place?" Red shook his head.

By this time, my mind was working again. "Suppose," I said, "we brought you a small bucket. And a bunch of plastic bags. You could just fill one of the bags for us every day. And we could take it to the compost heap."

I could see that Red didn't like the idea. But he is a nice guy, and he gave in. "Just one thing," he warned. "If there is any mess — or any other kind of trouble — it will be on your heads. Understand?"

By that time, I would have agreed to anything. In fact, we even talked him into giving us some of the leftovers from one of his barrels.

Half an hour later, Lily had finished the last
scrap. Then she stretched out on the floor and
started to sleep.

Susan and I felt happy, too.

We had taken care of the problem. We had it
made. At least that's what we thought until we got
home.

Mom, Dad, and Pete were watching TV. The
Sunday afternoon news. It was bad news. The
announcer was talking about Lily!

CHAPTER 5

"There is still no news about Lily, the missing lion," the announcer was saying. "Lily disappeared during a riot in Millburg, Friday night. Officials are looking for her in four counties. Her owner, Fearless Freddie, has offered a reward of one hundred dollars for Lily's return.

Dad made a face. "That's all we need in this town. A wild lion running around."

"She's not wild," I said. "You should have seen her at the circus. She could hardly stand up."

"That's right," Pete said.

Dad shook his head. "If she couldn't stand up, then how did she run away?"

"Maybe she fell out of her cage—from weakness," said Susan.

I thought that was a good answer. But Dad turned it around. "If she's that weak, then she never left the county," he said. "She has to still be in Millburg."

"Well, if she's here, then they will find her," I said, hoping he would stop talking about it.

But he didn't stop talking about it. "If any of you see her, don't count on her weakness," he warned. "A hungry lion will do anything for food. And you know what they eat, don't you? MEAT!"

I knew better than to argue about that. Luckily, I didn't have to. Mom said, "Could I please hear the rest of the news?"

That gave me a chance to slip out of the room. A minute later, Susan joined me in the kitchen. We were worried. We could see that Lily was more of a problem than we wanted to admit. Sooner or later, somebody would find out about her. And then Fearless Freddie would get her back.

We just couldn't bear that. So we made up our minds to be careful. And, for the next few days, things seemed to be working out.

I got the bucket and some plastic bags for Red. On my way home from school, I collected the leftovers "for the compost heap." I hid them in the tool shed overnight. And every morning, on the way to school, Susan and I stopped by the cave.

We brought Lily her food. We also brought her a can, which we filled with fresh water from the river. That way, she wouldn't ever have to go out and take a chance on being seen.

There was still one more thing that we did for security. As we left the cave, I put a pile of rocks around the opening, so that no one would spot it. Lily didn't seem to mind.

By the end of the week, we began to notice something funny. Lily wasn't eating all her food. She certainly wasn't chomping it down anymore. She would pick at it, eating some of the things, leaving the rest.

I wondered if she was getting sick.

"I don't think she is so hungry anymore," said Susan. "That Freddie was starving her. And now, since she has been eating every day. . . . "

I wanted to believe it. But I had a feeling that it was something else. The things Lily was leaving were vegetables and bread. I wondered if she really missed having meat.

On Saturday morning, Susan and I left the house early. I wanted to see Lily before going to play ball. When we got to the cave, my heart jumped. The rocks I had piled up in front of it were all pushed away.

We went in and turned on the flashlight. Lily was there! What a relief! But when we dumped the bag of leftovers in front of her, I knew something was wrong. Lily didn't even go near them.

We turned the light around the cave, trying to

find out what was wrong. For the first time, I noticed that those leftovers from Red's Diner were piling up in one corner. Without even planning it, we were making a compost heap! Right there in the cave.

"We'll have to get rid of this stuff," I told Susan. "It's going to start to smell. We'll have to come back after dark and bury it."

While we were talking and shining the light, I saw something that gave me goose pimples. I went a little closer to the pile of old food. There were feathers mixed up with the leftovers!

Susan spotted them too. "Where did those come

from?" she asked, saying out loud exactly what I was thinking. "They couldn't have come from the diner."

I grabbed a stick and started poking around. Then I saw something that almost made me flip. It looked like the foot of a chicken, only bigger. It turned out to be a duck's foot!

Without saying a word to each other, Susan and I both guessed the truth. Lily had wanted meat — just like Ollie had told us. And she had pushed her way out of the cave and gone hunting. She had caught one of the ducks and made a meal of it!

We had a real problem on our hands. If Lily

started hunting for meat, somebody was bound to see her. Besides, we couldn't let her go around killing the ducks.

"I don't understand it," said Susan. "She seemed to like those leftovers for the first few days."

"Maybe it's because — like you said — she was really starving. Or maybe there was more meat in them."

"If we could get some meat to mix in with the other stuff, maybe she would be satisfied."

Maybe she would. The trouble was...meat cost too much!

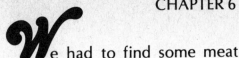e had to find some meat for Lily. I didn't go to the ball game. I went home and got some more of my paper-route money. We bought a lot of hamburger. Then we mixed it with the other leftovers. That seemed to keep Lily happy over the weekend.

On Monday we had a new plan.

Susan took over my paper route after school. I got another job I started delivering orders for Mr. Heinz, the butcher.

Mr. Heinz was a nice, friendly man. I told him I had to help feed a friend's dog.

"What kind of dog is he?" asked Mr. Heinz.

"A Great Dane," I said. That was the biggest dog I could think of.

Mr. Heinz's eyes opened wide with surprise. "Those dogs eat five pounds of meat a day. That's a lot of meat. Do you know how many orders you will have to deliver?"

"My friend is also chipping in," I said. "Besides, this dog isn't so fussy. She doesn't have to eat the best meat."

"It won't be the best meat," said Mr. Heinz. "But I can help you out. There are all sorts of odds and ends that I throw away. If you don't mind doing a little work, you can have them free. You have to trim them."

Mind? He should have known how happy those words made me feel!

Mr. Heinz showed me what to do. The scraps of meat had to be trimmed from the waste. It wasn't hard. Mr. Heinz's knives were sharp. But you had to be careful. "Your finger could wind up in the Great Dane's dinner plate," Mr. Heinz warned me.

He also showed me how to use the meat grinder. It was easy because it was electric. At the end of each day, I had two or three pounds of chopped meat for Lily. Free! Sometimes I would buy another pound of meat, too. That made Lily even happier.

Once again, Susan and I thought we had it made.

We kept feeding Lily the leftovers from Red's. And the meat from Mr. Heinz. We put more rocks in front of the cave. That way we made sure

Lily stayed inside. And she was always there the next day.

But we had to do a lot of quick thinking.

Somebody saw that Susan was delivering papers for me.

And someone else told my mother that I was working for Mr. Heinz.

Somehow, we always came up with an answer. It wasn't easy, but we didn't mind. Lily was like an old friend now. She was like a dog that we had had around for years. As long as we kept her happy,

Fearless Freddie wouldn't get his hands on her.

We made only one mistake. We forgot to watch out for Pete.

Pete, as I said before, is nine. But he is pretty smart. He didn't say anything. He just kept listening and watching. And he guessed that Susan and I were up to something.

I guess he felt left out of things. Or maybe he saw certain looks between me and Susan. All I can say for sure is this: We didn't know Pete was spying on us — until it was too late.

CHAPTER 7

It was near the end of our second week of caring for Lily. Friday morning, to be exact.

Susan and I went through our usual act.

I left for school first. I stopped at the shed to pick up Lily's food. I walked one block south—toward my school. Then I turned right and walked two blocks. There I turned right again and walked north for one block. That was the way to Susan's school. Susan and I met at that corner.

We went to the park, heading straight for the cave. We pushed away the rocks and crawled in. Lily was waiting for us. She purred and licked our hands. She acted like a pet.

Susan opened the bag, and Lily dug in. I got her water pail and put fresh water in it.

We stayed there a while, watching Lily chomp away. She sure liked what we were feeding her now. And she looked a lot different. She wasn't that poor, scrawny lion we first saw in the circus.

Her bones were not showing. Her fur was nice and smooth. Susan and I took turns brushing it, to make it look more shiny.

Then it was time to go to school. We said goodbye to Lily and left the cave. We put the rocks back in front of the opening. Then we walked along the narrow path by the brook, and started across the park.

We had gone about 50 yards, when something made me stop. To this day, I still don't know what it was.

Susan looked at me, as if to ask, "What's the matter, Glenn?" Then, her glance followed mine. We both nearly fainted at what we saw.

Pete was making his way along the edge of the brook. He was heading for the cave. In fact, he was already in front of it. He was pushing the rocks away.

Susan was about to yell out at him. But I put my hand over her mouth. Susan looked at me as though I were crazy. But I kept my hand over her mouth and pointed. Between us and Pete was old Ollie Olson!

Susan and I ran and hid behind some trees. We watched, not knowing what else to do. Pete pushed the rocks away. Then he stood there for a minute. It seemed like a year.

He peeked into the hole. We could tell he was afraid to crawl in. Then he stood back up. If only he would leave before Ollie saw him. We held our breath and prayed.

At that moment, Lily stuck her nose out. She was just being curious.

Pete backed away so fast that he landed in the water. Surprised and afraid, he screamed. And Lily, more afraid than Pete, let out a roar!

Ollie stopped in his tracks.

Susan and I didn't know what to do. We knew that Pete would be all right. The water isn't very deep. Besides, Ollie had already spotted him and Lily. And he was heading for the cave!

"Get back on dry land, son!" called Ollie. "And get out of the way. I'll take care of that lion."

But Lily was taking care of herself! She came charging out of the cave. She raced across the park. She ran up a hill and headed for a place where the trees were thick. Then she was gone.

Susan and I couldn't believe our eyes. After all the trouble we had taken to protect Lily. Now Pete had gone and blown the whole thing!

I couldn't really blame Pete. He just wanted to know what was going on. And I couldn't be mad at

Ollie. He was only doing what he thought was right.

The person I hated was Fearless Freddie. He beat his animals and wouldn't feed them. Now he would do it again to Lily. And there was no way to stop him.

As Ollie went off to chase Lily, we ran back to Pete. Pete was in tears. He was soaking wet. He felt bad about giving away our secret. At the same time, he was sore because we had not let him in on it.

He kept trying to say all these things at once. I made him calm down.

"Look," I told him. "The most important thing is to go home and change clothes."

Pete looked as though I was sending him to jail. "What will I tell Mom?" he said.

"Maybe she won't be home," answered Susan. "She usually goes to the market around this time."

"But what if she is?"

"Make up a story," I said. "Any story. Tell her some bully turned the water hose on you. Tell her anything. But don't mention Lily!"

Pete nodded. But I could see that he didn't understand how important it was. "Let's get out of the park," I told him and Susan. "Ollie might be coming back."

On the way, I explained to Pete. "You see, people think that Lily's dangerous. That's what

Fearless Freddie wants them to believe."

"But—it's not true?" asked Pete.

"Of course not!" said Susan. "She wouldn't hurt a fly. And we should know. We have been in that cave with her every day for almost two weeks."

Pete's eyes opened so wide I thought they would pop out of his head. "Every day for two weeks!"

Susan nodded. "That's right."

"Then—if she's not dangerous, why shouldn't people know?" he asked.

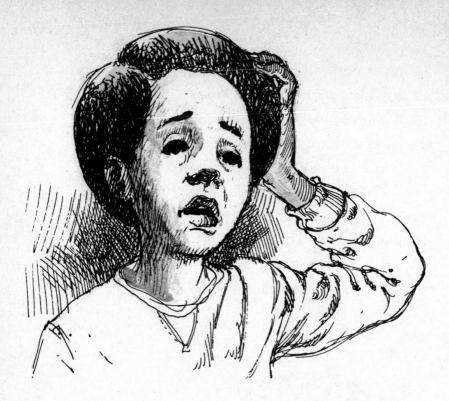

"For two reasons," I answered. "First, they wouldn't believe it. Second, the more people who know about it, the better are Freddie's chances of getting her back."

Pete looked more mixed up than ever. "But how can you stop him now?"

"You go home and let me worry about that!" I yelled. Pete winced and took off.

Then I told Susan to go on to her school. And I went to mine. I felt rotten about everything, especially about yelling at poor Pete. But the reason I lost my temper was that I was worried. I didn't know the answer to his questions any more than he did.

CHAPTER 8

I went to school. It was the worst morning of my life. I went from one class to the next. I didn't see or hear a thing. All I could think about was Lily. Did she get caught? Did she get away? Suppose she was hit by a car while running across the street?

I tried to think what might have happened. I knew she could get away from Ollie. He was pretty old and slow on his feet. But I knew Ollie wouldn't give up. He would call the police, or whoever you call in the case of a runaway lion.

I thought about it and thought about it. But I knew what would happen. Lily would be trapped. Then she would be handed over to Fearless Fred-

die. She would be sent back to that circus. And she would get beaten and whipped.

It was almost lunch time. I was in my Geography class. But my mind was . . . I don't know where. I had no idea that the teacher was talking to me. Some kid poked me in the ribs.

"Hey, Glenn!" he whispered. "Wake up, man!"

I sat up. The teacher was looking at me. She seemed very annoyed. "Thank you for your attention, Glenn," she said. "Now will you please tell us what is the capital of Mississippi?"

I saw her lips moving. And I heard the words. But my head was so mixed up, I didn't understand what she was saying.

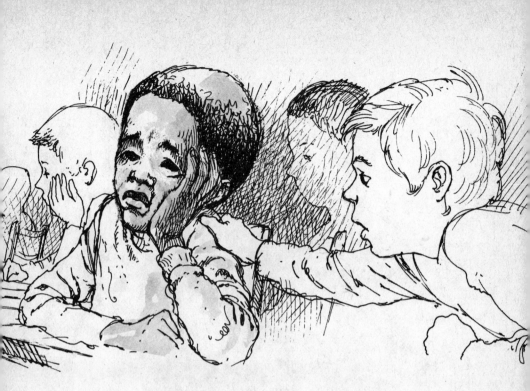

I could feel my face turning red. The whole class was staring at me. I couldn't stand it. So I turned and looked out the window.

"You won't find the answer out there," said the teacher.

This time, I heard her. But it was like in a dream. I had the feeling that it was a dream. If it wasn't, then it was the craziest thing that ever happened.

I kept looking out that window. And something outside was looking at me! Would you ever believe what it was? That's right! It was Lily!

All of a sudden, Lily let out a roar. And I knew it wasn't a dream. So did the rest of the class. The whole school, for that matter.

I opened the window and climbed out. It seemed that the whole town was out there. Everyone . . . except Lily. She had taken off again.

Nobody went back to school that day. All the stores in Millburg closed. The only thing on everybody's mind was Lily. Most of the people seemed half scared to death. The rest were anxious to catch her. I guess they were all after that reward.

So there was a "lion hunt" underway. Policemen and firemen took the lead. Ollie Olson, "the animal expert," helped out. There were lots of other people helping out, too.

I spotted Red from the diner. And I saw Mr. Heinz, the butcher, in the crowd, too. But I didn't let them see me. I ducked away, and headed for the park.

I went straight to the cave—where else?

But the opening was really blocked now. There was a rock in front of it. It must have weighed more than 100 pounds. I figured that Ollie had taken care of that.

I waited around, wondering what to do. Then Susan came along. She had heard the news at her school.

She saw the big rock in front of the cave. She knew what that meant. As we were talking about it, we heard a loud roar. It came from the crowd of "lion hunters." They were heading our way.

Then there was another roar. This time it was

Lily. She was running away from the crowd. She headed for the cave. But she stopped when she saw it was blocked. Then she spotted us. She looked at us with her big sad eyes. It was as if she were begging us to save her.

The "lion hunters" were closing in. Some of them were carrying ropes and poles. One woman was waving a pitchfork. I patted Lily lightly to let her know how we felt. Then I gave her a hard slap on the back. I yelled, "Take off, Lily! Go!"

Lily went — like a shot. She jumped over the big rock. Then she raced down the narrow path by the brook. She followed it to where the brook flows into a culvert. The culvert is a round pipe, made of concrete. It's about six feet wide. It starts at the edge of the park, then disappears underground. Lily disappeared with it.

The crowd came running up to the edge of the brook and stopped. Everybody looked at the leaders: Police Chief Chester, firemen Ford, and Ollie Olson.

"What do we do now?" a man asked.

"We're going to bag that lion," said Chief Chester.

"Right!" said firemen Ford.

"Hooray!" yelled the crowd.

Ollie stood there a minute. He scratched his head. "OK," he said slowly to the chief. "But . . . how are we going to bag her?"

Chief Chester puffed up his chest. "I've got a
strategy," he said. "A plan." He pointed to the big
concrete pipe. "That culvert connects with all the
sewers of Millburg," he said. "They all lead to the
filtering plant, at the other end, on the river. If we
block this pipe, then she will be trapped
underground. And she won't be able to get out
unless we let her. No way! All we have to do is pick
the right spot and grab her."

he "lion hunters" went to work. Fireman Ford and his men got a big net. They tied it around the mouth of the culvert. Lily was bottled up.

Somebody went to the Town Hall to get a map of the sewers. Looking at the map, we could see that all the pipes were connected. But each one ran into a dead end on one side. On the other, they all emptied into the main line. That line went to the filtering plant.

It seemed easy to trap Lily, but it turned out to be a lot harder than it looked. Lily could be in any one of those pipes. And there were lots of them.

Chief Chester told us his plan. It went like this:

To search each pipe, between the dead end and the main sewer line. If Lily wasn't in it, they would close off that pipe. They would use another net. Little by little, they would close in on Lily.

A lot of nets were put onto the fire truck. Then the hunters started opening manholes, pulling off those round iron covers. They would shine a light down, and if Lily wasn't in it, they would drop a net across the opening. That would keep her out.

It was a good plan, I guess. Lily would be trapped, but it was going to take a while. Susan and I followed the fire truck all afternoon. During all that time, no one saw anything of Lily. We went home for dinner.

We had to let Mom and Dad know where we were. We had not been home since we had left for school that morning. Besides, I had an idea of my own. It needed a little working out.

Mom and Dad were worried. They had heard about the wild lion on the loose. I told them how Lily was trapped underground and couldn't get away. I really worked on them, without letting them catch on. By the time dinner was over, they were hooked. It was they who said let's go see how the "lion hunt" was coming along.

We all went out together. Pete went, too. Half the town was in the streets. It wasn't hard to find out where the hunt was. And everybody seemed to have the latest reports.

Mrs. Williams, a neighbor, told us that the whole east half of the system was blocked off. "They are working on the west side now."

"Has anyone seen the lion?" asked Dad.

"Well, they spotted her a couple of times. On the 'catwalks.' Seems lions don't like to get wet, if they can help it."

"What are 'catwalks?'" Dad wanted to know.

"Narrow ledges along the sides of the pipe," Mrs. Williams explained. "The water runs down the ditch, in the middle. The 'catwalks' are for workmen to stand on, when they have to go down inside. You know — to make repairs or clean out ditches that are stopped up."

Dad thought that was a great joke. "They build sewers with 'catwalks.' And who walks on them? A wild cat! I tell you — "

Before he could tell anyone anything, a loud shout went up for some people near the fire truck. We all ran over to find out what was going on.

Fireman Ford had just spotted Lily. She was on the "catwalk" in the main sewer line.

He called to Chief Chester to throw him a net. The chief grabbed one. But, in the excitement, his feet caught in the net. He tripped and fell into the manhole. To make matters worse, he landed on fireman Ford, and the two of them ended up in the dirty ditch water!

At the same time, Lily raced by them — along the "catwalk" — heading for the culvert!

People crowded around the manhole to help pull the two men out. That was my chance . . . to try my plan.

I got Pete and Susan, and we left. There wasn't time to tell them my plan. I just told them what to do.

"You, Pete," I said. "I want you to go straight home and — "

"I always get left out!" Pete cut in.

"You're not being left out!" I told him. "You've got something important to do there! Now listen. I want you to go the tool shed behind the garage. Make some room in there — for Lily. But be quiet about it. No noise. And don't put on any lights. You got that?"

Pete nodded. He felt good. He was in on things now. But he had a question. "Should I come back here?"

"No, just wait there. Now get going, man!"

Pete took off on the run.

"Come on, Susan!" I yelled, heading for the park. Susan knew better than to waste time asking questions. But when we got to the culvert, and I pulled out my pocket knife, she couldn't believe her eyes.

"If they ever find out . . . " she said.

"Let's just hope that they don't," I said. I cut the ropes that held the net. "And let's hope that Lily guesses what we're up to."

Of course, Lily guessed! As the net dropped into the water, Lily stuck her head out. We called her name, and she came out.

We led her through the park, petting her.
"Everything will be all right," I kept telling her.
"Don't be scared." I wondered if she knew how
scared I was.

We took the long way home, cutting through
back alleys. We got her into the shed, told her to
be quiet, then closed the door.

As Susan, Pete, and I went into the house, Pete
gave me a funny look. "What are we going to do
now?" he asked.

"What do you mean?" said Susan.

"Well, she will be all right in there for tonight," said Pete. "But what about tomorrow? And the day after? She can't just stay there forever."

"Let's worry about tomorrow . . . tomorrow," I told him. "By tomorrow, they will call off that hunt. And we'll find a new place to keep her."

That's what I said. But it's not what I was thinking. I was thinking that Pete was right. I just couldn't bear to face the problem.

he way things turned out, I didn't have to face it. The problem faced me! I mean — it came straight to our house the next day!

The "lion hunt" went on all night. The next day it was called off. By morning, reporters from all over the state were in town. Lily was big news.

Somebody else was in town that morning. Fearless Freddie. He had heard about the "lion hunt." Freddie brought help. The kind of help no one else had.

Freddie and his men had come in a truck. There was a big cage on the back of it. In the cage was Louie. Louie was the other lion from the circus.

Freddie led Louie on a long, heavy leash. And Louie followed Lily's scent. They came right to our house.

A big crowd followed behind Freddie and Louie. People wanted to get Lily out of town. There was Chief Chester in front of the crowd. Fireman Ford and Ollie Olson were there, too. But there were also 500 men, women, and children. Mom almost passed out when she looked out the window.

Louie stopped and sniffed around. Then he headed for the little shed. Freddie opened the door. And Lily jumped out, roaring. For the first time since I saw her, she looked like a killer! She looked ready to kill Fearless Freddie!

Susan and I raced out of the house. Mom and Dad tried to call us back. But we kept going. We were not worried or afraid.

We went straight up to Lily and petted her. Freddie couldn't believe his eyes. But the minute he made a move toward her, she stiffened and growled. She also showed her teeth.

"This is ridiculous!" said Freddie. Then he turned to one of his men. Freddie grabbed a long whip. At the same time, he gave Louie's leash to the man.

Lily made a sound that I just can't describe. It had to be some kind of "lion talk." Because, in one second, Louie broke loose and moved over to Lily's side.

Now the crowd began to back away. They were worried. And somebody said out loud, "Those crazy kids will get us all killed!"

That was all Freddie needed to hear. He lifted his whip. Then he turned and faced the lions. Susan and I got right in front of them. Freddie turned to the crowd to say something. It looked as if we were going to have another riot!

Freddie was telling the crowd that we were crazy. That somebody was going to get hurt. That these lions were dangerous.

"You're a big fat liar!" I told him. I said it without even meaning to.

Freddie's mouth fell open. But no words came out of it. The crowd was quiet. Then Susan and I both told all the people what we knew about Lily. And we felt sure that it went for Louie, too. The proof of it was that we were standing right next to the lions. And they didn't look or sound mean at all. In fact, they were purring. Lily must have been telling Louie all about us.

Freddie glanced from us to the crowd. Then he

looked at us again. A look came into his eyes. "Do you kids want these lions?" he said. "I'll sell them to you. A thousand dollars, for the pair!"

The crowd began to buzz with excitement. Chief Chester came over to join us.

"The man has a point," the chief said. "Those are his lions."

"But he beats them," said Susan. "And he doesn't feed them. They don't belong with a man like that. They belong in a zoo."

"Well," said Freddie, "you got a zoo here in town? I'll sell them to your zoo. Same price."

It was beginning to look like a standoff. One of those arguments where no one loses or wins. Then

I spotted Judge Jonas in the crowd. All at once I had another idea.

I asked Chief Chester to come closer. For a few seconds, I had the feeling that he was scared of Lily and Louie. But he couldn't let the crowd know that. So he came over.

He bent down and I whispered in his ear. Then he stood up. He walked over to the judge. Soon, he and the judge were back with us. They turned and faced Freddie.

"This town doesn't have a zoo," said the judge. "But we might start one. It could be in the park. These two lions would be a beginning. We would also need your cages. We'll offer you a thousand dollars for the whole lot."

"Well, I'm not going to argue for a few more dollars," said Freddie. I could tell from the look on his face that he knew he was robbing us.

That look went away when Judge Jonas tapped him on the shoulder. "However," said the judge, "there is something else. I have hundreds of witnesses. They can prove that you were cruel to your animals. On the night of the Grand Opening, to be exact. That is a criminal offense!"

He stopped. And we all saw Freddie turn green. Then the judge went on. "I could ask the chief to arrest you. Then I would try you and fine you. A thousand dollars, or a thousand days in jail. Or you can turn over the lions and the cages to Mr. Olson."

Freddie started to say something. Judge Jonas cut him off. "If you give us more trouble, the fine will be more. Take my advice and get out of town fast. And be careful how you treat those tigers in your act."

Freddie started to slink away.

"I'll be in touch with authorities in other towns where you perform. And they will see to it that you treat your animals better," the judge said.

Well, that is how the zoo in Millburg Park got started. It seems hard to believe that it was only a few months ago. Since then, we held a fund drive to raise money for big, roomy cages. And we now have a few more animals.

Our favorites, of course, are Lily and Louie. Sometimes, when no one's around, Ollie lets Susan and me feed them. And I'll tell you this. They get first-class horsemeat. Ten to twelve pounds each. Every day.